W9-BSL-834

Monkey: Not Ready for bedtime

Marc Brown

Alfred A. Knopf 🐎 New York

CHICAGO HEIGHTS PUBLIC LIBRARY

3 1539 00267 0115

But Monkey couldn't fall asleep.

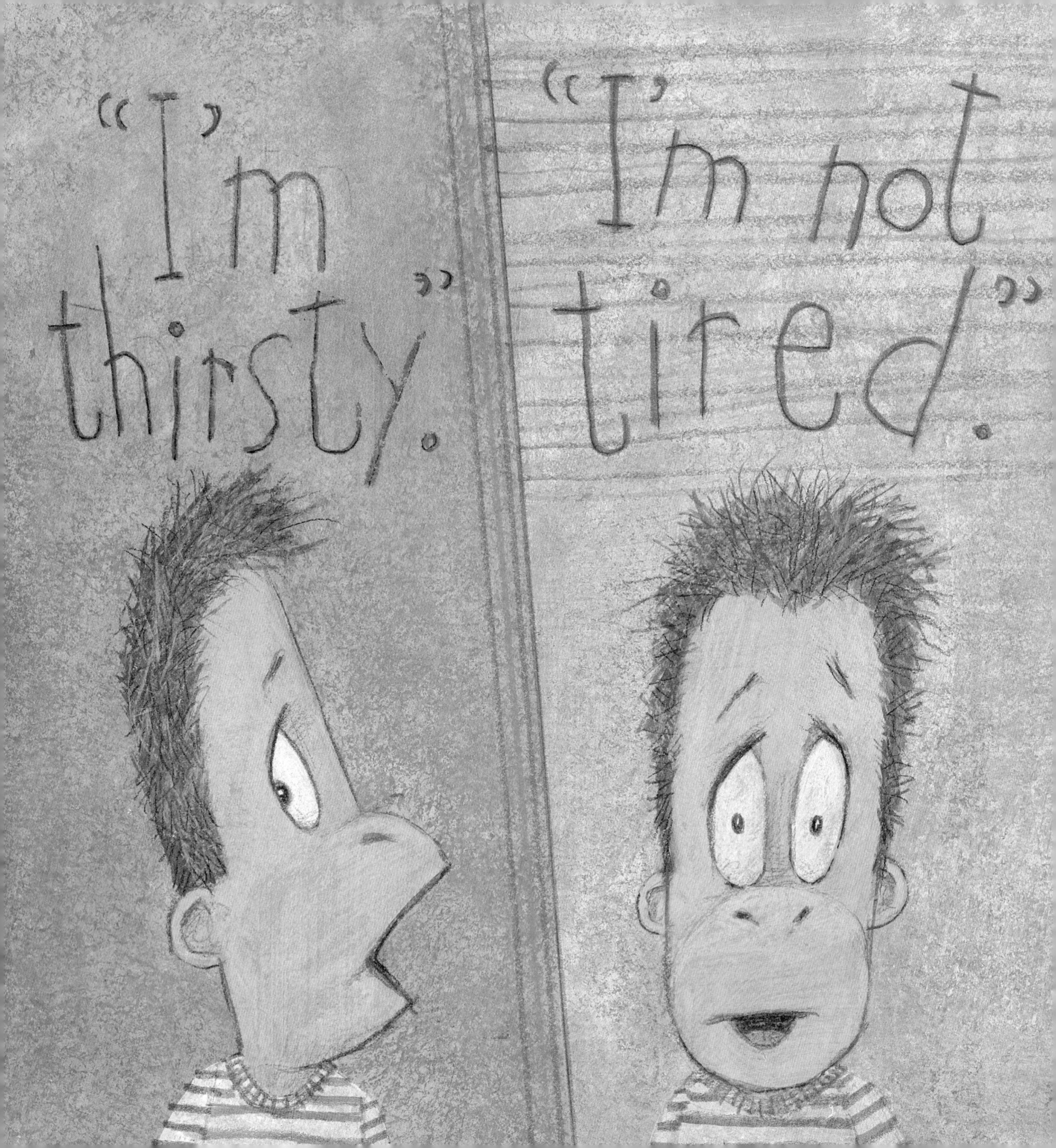
"I'm thirsty."
"I'm not tired."

Daddy gives
Monkey
a backrub.

But every night
it's the same problem.
Monkey is just **not**
ready for bed.

It's no fun
being tired at school.

At home.

But then Monkey's brother has an idea.

"Some people count things to fall asleep. Find something you really like and count it slowly."

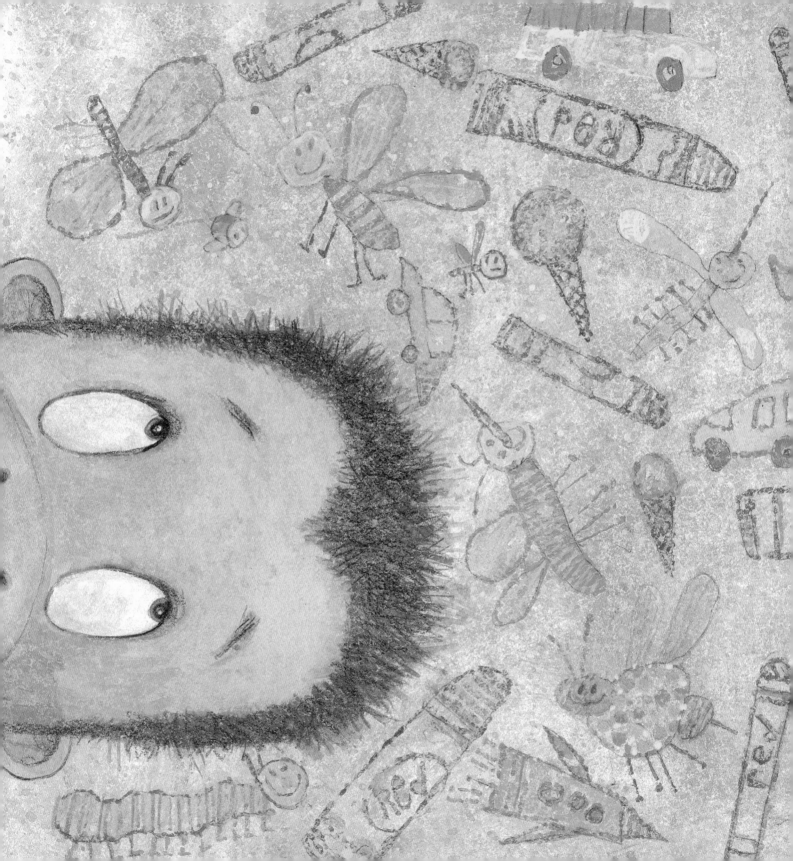

That night, Monkey tries counting bugs.

Red crayons.

Toys.

Raspberry ice cream cones.

But it wasn't working.

And then he
remembers.
"I LOVE dinosaurs!
He begins counting slowly.

One Allosaurus.

Two Iguanodons.

Three Triceratops... This was fun.

He flies with the Dimorphodons.

He rocks with T. rex.

All the
dinosaurs
join in.
It's a dinosaur
jamboree.

He scoots down a Diplodocus.

He races with the Gallimimus.

And before long, it's no surprise that they all get very, very, very sleepy.

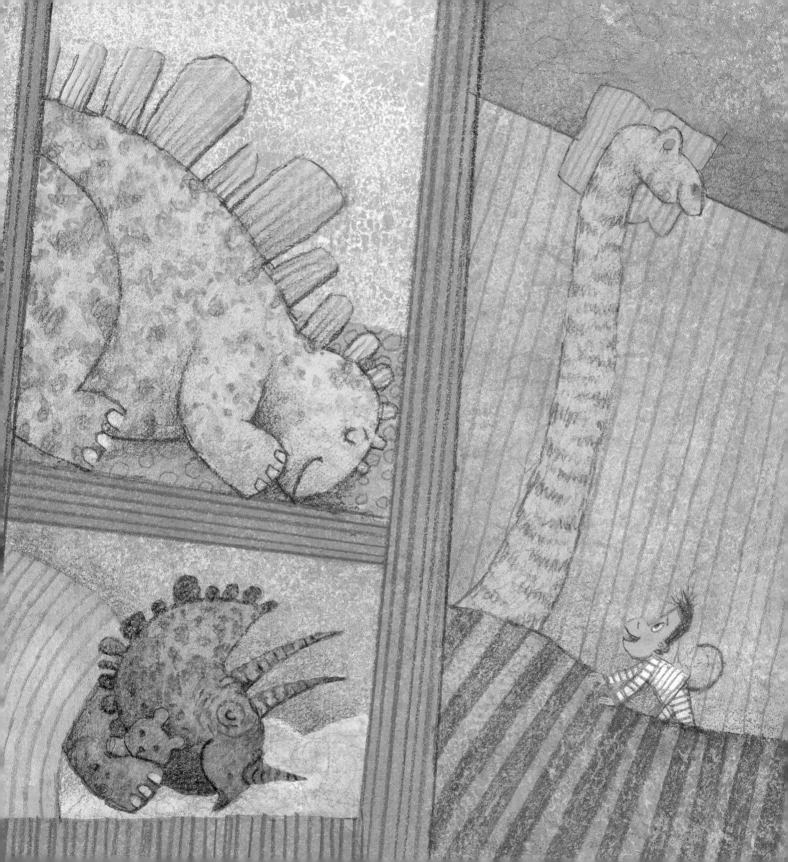

Monkey, too.

·for·

○Jenny and Isabel ○

THIS IS A BORZOI BOOK PUBLISHED BY ALFRED A. KNOPF

Copyright © 2017 by Marc Brown

All rights reserved. Published in the United States by Alfred A. Knopf, an imprint of Random House Children's Books, a division of Penguin Random House LLC, New York.

Knopf, Borzoi Books, and the colophon are registered trademarks of Penguin Random House LLC.

Visit us on the Web! randomhousekids.com

Educators and librarians, for a variety of teaching tools, visit us at RHTeachersLibrarians.com

Library of Congress Cataloging-in-Publication Data is available upon request.
ISBN 978-1-101-93761-7 (trade) — ISBN 978-1-101-93762-4 (lib. bdg.) —
ISBN 978-1-101-93763-1 (ebook)

The text of this book was created by hand by Marc Brown, accompanied by a few typeset bits in Elephant.
The illustrations were created using colored pencils and gouache.

MANUFACTURED IN CHINA
September 2017
10 9 8 7 6 5 4 3 2 1
First Edition

Random House Children's Books supports the First Amendment and celebrates the right to read.

CHICAGO HEIGHTS PUBLIC LIBRARY

E

Caudipteryx

Triceratops

Quetzalcoatlus

Iguanodon

Stegosaurus

T.rex

Zuhiceratops

Hesperornis